Baby Loves

Michael Lawrence

Illustrated by Adrian Reynolds

DORLING KINDERSLEY

NEW YORK • LONDON • STUTTGART • MOSCOW

Baby loves

Mummy and

Daddy more than anything in the world. Except...

Breakfast

Baby loves Breakfast
more than anything
in the world except...

Teddy

Baby loves Teddy more than anything in the world except...

Puss

Baby loves Puss more
than anything in the
world except...

Slippers

Baby loves Slippers more than anything in the world except...

Flowers

Baby loves Flowers
more than anything
in the world except...

Baby loves Granny more than anything in the world except...

Hat

Baby loves Hat
more than
anything in
the world
except...

Baby loves Sunshine more than anything in the world except...

Rain

Baby loves Rain more than anything in the world except...

Drum

Baby loves Drum more than
anything in the world except…

Duck

Baby loves Duck more than

anything in the world except...

Baby loves
Bathtime
more than
anything in
the world
except...

And Mummy and Daddy
love Baby more
than anything
in the world except...

No.

Mummy and

Daddy love

Baby

more than anything

in the world...

Anything at all!

For Jemima and Max Gee,
proud new parents M.L.
For Julian, Isabel and Joseph A.R.

A Dorling Kindersley Book

First published in Great Britain in 1998
by Dorling Kindersley Limited,
9 Henrietta Street, London WC2E 8PS
Text copyright © 1998 Michael Lawrence
Illustrations © 1998 Adrian Reynolds
The author's and illustrator's moral rights have been asserted.
Visit us on the World Wide Web at
http://www.dk.com
A CIP catalogue record for this book is available from the British Library.
ISBN 0 7513 7144 0 (Hardback)
ISBN 0 7513 7181 5 (Paperback)
Colour reproduction by Dot Gradations Ltd.
Printed in Hong Kong by Wing King Tong